Dear Jillian,

You are going to do amazing things in life – work hard and never give up.

[illegible signature]

MARJANAH'S

DNADVENTURE

Written by Margaret Bruce

Illustrated by Xhe Titi

In loving memory of my brother Morgan.

A part of you will always be with me, and a part of me will always be with you.

We share the same DNA after all…

For Mona

TABLE OF CONTENTS

CHAPTER 1

FIRST DAYS

Although it was early for September, rusty orange leaves were already falling outside the classroom windows. Clinging to the glass were apples decorated with the student's names in big sharpie ink.

Fall had arrived, and third

grade was already shaking up to be even more interesting than second. Arvand sat in the back of the classroom, wondering where on Earth Marjanah was.

"MarJOHNnuh? Is there a Marjowannah present?" Silence. *Crickets.*

The kids sat in their desks wide-eyed, staring ahead as their new third grade teacher tried not to completely butcher their names while taking attendance. Some of the kids with spring birthdays disdainfully shook their heads. They thought they were so much older than everyone else, and therefore brilliant.

Marjanah popped through the door, huge clear framed glasses resting atop her nose and a bright purple backpack slung over one shoulder with her long dark hair set into a loose braid. She attempted to slink to the back desk, so aggravated that her dad had dropped her off late on his way to work this early in the year.

On my first day and everything! she thought, as her cheeks turned more pink than tan.

"Ahhh, you must be Marjoannuh!" the teacher, Mr. Chaplan cried a little too triumphantly. Marjanah was used to having to sound her name out for people, and the first day of school was never an exception.

"Excuse me Mr. Chaplan, it is actually pronounced Mar Jon Ah. And my last name is Jalali – Jah-lolly." She gave a smile that looked more like a wince and continued to the back where Arvand was already seated.

"Well perfect! M.J. it is."

"Ugghhh," sighed Marjanah under her breath. Mr. Chaplan winked and then with a little clickety-clack on his computer, was finally ready to begin the day. "Who is ready for a get to know you activity?"

Mr. Chaplan asked, as he began handing out worksheets. Arvand waved his hand and invited Marjanah to the seat next to him. “Here we go…” he murmured.

CHAPTER 2

GEERLKS UNITE!

Last year, Marjanah and her two best friends had been the perfect trifecta. They were like the three musketeers, but smarter and multi-cultural – and, well, girls. Olivia was an amazing engineer. . .err future engineer, we should say.

She was a total gear-head (her dad's words not hers) who loved to build robots and make things come to life. Give her a carton of baking soda, a battery and two wires, and she could give you at least five different items that either explode or begin talking (sometimes both) in less than 20 minutes.

Then there was Myah. She was a bonafide geek extraordinaire, and proud of it. Unlike Marjanah, who only pretended to have glasses, Myah had them for real and they looked great on her. She had chosen bright red frames to bring out her beautiful dark skin.

Rumor had it Myah was the only student at Shakerside Elementary who had known how to do long division since the first grade...with her eyes closed and one hand behind her back. "For the record, that's what a rock star genius looks like, by the way!" she used to say as patted herself on the back after nailing a 4th grade story problem.

The girls had been really competitive in Ms. Barwhani's first grade class, but in the second grade, they had become best friends. "Geerlks unite!" they would shout, as they ran home from school. That was the best blend of girls and geeks they could agree upon; geerlks—a work in progress indeed.

Everyone knew they were best friends, but their role as geerlks wasn't totally official in their mind until they won the ***Top Prize*** at Shakerside Elementary Science Fair at the end of second grade.

It was last year at the Science Fair that their win sealed the deal: they knew they were the most super cool, smart girls the world could find.

They went home that perfectly

clear, blue skied afternoon, riding high with big smiles, their calculators clicking and backpacks bulging. "My house. 3 o'clock. Ice pops for everyone!" Olivia cheered as they left school. Everything was going so smoothly...until later that afternoon.

CHAPTER 3

NERD ALERT

Marjanah remembered it like it was yesterday, even though more than a year had passed. It all started innocently enough, with the girls wearing their blue ribbons proudly on their shirts. Mr. McKee, the bus driver, congratulated them as they hopped on. "Good work young ladies. You should be proud of yourselves, workin' so hard and all, must really be going places. . .like home on this bus!" He laughed loudly to himself.

Myah said thank you and kind of rolled her eyes as they made their way to the back of the bus. That Mr. McKee was perhaps the corniest adult they knew, and they knew <u>a lot</u> of corny adults. But they still loved him, even though he laughed exuberantly at his own jokes.

"WEE WOO, WEE WOO! Nerd alert! Nerd alert!" they heard Josh Korben call from the back of the bus. He continued to make those terrible siren sounds while pretending to move like a robot. Josh and Trina were the two coolest kids in school, according to themselves. Both had soft straight hair, eyes like a cool lake and always wore the coolest clothes.

Trina was not far behind with her oh so witty response: "Girls, congratulations on your prize – your prize of being the top dweebs of the entire school, that is! Oh, and nice fake glasses Marjanah. Everyone knows you passed your eye exam no problem."

"These are totally real glass!" Marjanah called back before

muttering "but who said you need a prescription to be real?" under her breath. Olivia cut her off and took the place in front of her. "Trina, you really don't know what you're talking about. Our science project was amazing and one day we'll go to college and we'll be even more amazing."

"Ohhhhhhh smarty college pants" Trina said in a singsong voice. "I am sooooo jealous of your nerdiness. Jeez, you guys don't even act like girls or do things you're supposed to do, like wear skirts and text. You only care about running out in the field and doing 'experiments,'" she said with her fingers held up, as if experiments were not a real thing you could do.

"Sit down back there! Otherwise I'll turn this bus into *the Magic School Bus,*" Mr. McKee called out, while laughing to himself. Myah, Marjanah and Olivia quickly found open seats, with Myah in a three-seater to stay close to her friends. Olivia and Myah held their heads high. *They are so strong,* Marjanah thought. But inside, she felt a tiny crack pierce her heart.

She made a small wish to be different, a different person. Literally, anyone else would do.

But long, straight light colored hair just like Trina's would be a good start.

As the bus jangled along, the crack went from little to big. She wished not to have her lovely brown skin, have 20/20 vision, go to Mosque with her family, or love science and cats and other classically uncool things, that she *did* love with her whole heart. It was a big wish to be more like Trina and Josh and have normal lives like them.

Finally, it was the girls' stop. They got off the bus without saying a word. They walked the first block in silence and then

Myah stopped. "You guys—enough! This is ridiculous. We should be celebrating! We shouldn't be down in the dumps over what some half-lives think about us." "You know what? You're right!" Olivia piped in.

"Anyways, I think they're both missing an atom or two. We should not tolerate getting treated like that! We have rights too. Girls have rights to be who they want to be, and study what they want to study and be thought special and unique no matter what they look like."

Marjanah picked her head up. "EUREKA! I have a brilliant idea.

Girls have rights—GHR—it can be our new club! We can use it to work together and promote how special we are. We can do experiments together, write letters to state representatives and change the world!"

"Brilliant." Myah replied. "Welcome to the first official meeting of GHR." She winked, turned on her heel and headed up her family's driveway. That summer was off to a great start. The girls met almost daily to discover new things, perform science experiments and keep notes in their STEAM journal they shared.

STEAM, the acronym for science, technology, engineering, arts and mathematics was the thread that bound the girls together. Myah always joked it stood for super talented enlightened amazing models.

Then one day, Marjanah received an email. It was from Arvand.

Subject: Your club?

From: Arvand Patel

Hi Marjanah,

It's Arvand from school. I heard about your club with Myah and Olivia. Where do you perform experiments? I am kind of good at computers and writing code and stuff, and I'd like to join. When is the next meeting?

-Arvand

CHAPTER 4

AN A HA MOMENT

From back where their houses were, the meeting was just a twinkling light among the tall fir trees that grew beyond the field. Even if they saw the light, their parents would most likely not look twice – no one would have – because the light was so inconspicuous.

Only the most discerning eye would have been able to tell that this was their sacred and secret meeting spot.

Most typical kids would probably think the light was an oncoming car, or maybe, just maybe, someone on an evening stroll using a small flashlight or headlamp to guide her steps through the tall grass and small rolling hills.

The wind came with a bitter chill, and you could smell the smell of cold in the air, winter drawing was near. But Marjanah knew that at best it was a very distant glimmer of snow in the night sky.

The girls still had Halloween candy left over, so the reality of winter—and all the icicle-based experiments yet to be performed—had not yet occurred to them. The kids sat together in a circle. Pine needles, though softer than the hard ground below them, hardly provided enough cushioning, which is why Arvand had been tasked with bringing the blanket.

Spread beneath them was a rough woolen cloth, which Arvand had thought would be thick enough. It was mostly white, with some green, red and blue stripes. Myah had taken a box of granola and some carrots from her pantry to provide sustenance for the deep thinking that was sure to come at the 2nd annual meeting of the new and improved collective: KHR. Kids Have Rights.

"I'm so cold I can't even feel my butt," Olivia whispered smarmily as she grabbed for another carrot. "And what's up with this food, huh, health nut?" she said with a smiling glare in Myah's direction. "Hey, it was all I could manage to grab before my mom got suspicious. And look, you guys know I have to be back with my homework done and ready for dinner by 6:30 *SHARP*. My dad made it pretty clear he was *not* kidding last time."

"Well," Olivia said, "get ready to fall in love. with. me. For bringing the best possible treats." She stuck her hand into the pocket of her hoodie and started unloading sour gummies, four chocolate kisses and a pack of super-duper-double chew bubble gum. "JACKPOT!" Arvand called and grabbed a gummy.

"Ahem. This has been a real hoot, but don't act like this is a typical kids club house, guys. This is the 2nd official meeting of

KHR. We're so glad you could join us Arvand," Marjanah began. Meanwhile, Olivia sat beside Marjanah wagging her finger, lip-synching Marjanah's meeting introduction, and pushing up her pretend glasses.

"It used to be just Girls Have Rights, because you know we got tired of being teased for being amazing at math and science."

"And engineering!" Olivia blurted out.

"That's right, Olivia, of course. Everyone thinks we should only care about writing and playing dress up and house like we're babies.

They think we should just be glued to our phones and tablets, as if Einstein would ever be caught dead slinging maniacal birds into pumpkins! Well, we're not like that. We're here today to come up with the world's most amazing, most fantastic, supercalifragilisticexpealido--"

"Calm down there, cowgirl!" Myah blurted out.

"Ahem, most amazing new experiment the world has ever seen." Marjanah continued.

The children sat in a circle, staring at one another. The light was growing dim from beyond the enclosure of the fir trees. All of a sudden, *crrrrruuuuuunch*! Ol[illegible] snapped into one of the carrots. Everyone turned, their eyes laser beams shooting at her. "Sorry guys! Just trying to lighten the mood here a little bit."

"Well, thanks for letting me join your club. I can write code like nobody's business, but just because I'd rather do that than play soccer, the other kids pick on me. Even my dad says I'm not athletic enough. I'm excited to find out more about this experiment, Marjanah."

"Get this--ancient legend has it that you can travel through time and space through a method called

Astral Projection. Anyone can do it! You just meditate and then think of where you want to go and zoom! You will be there, with your spirit and your body connected by an invisible chord that might snap you back at any moment." Marjanah explained. "Like a jet pack?" Arvand wondered aloud. "Precisely," Marjanah quickly followed.

"Well… this just got super weird." Olivia whispered.

Myah, forever the realist, began, "Hang on one minute there, oh mystic Marjanah. This whole thing is not scientific at all. In fact, it sounds like Peter Pan ate one too many pixie sticks and has officially gone off the deep end! And what do you mean, ancient legend? Wikipedia does not qualify as ancient or legend, you know."

"Yeah well, I knew you guys wouldn't believe me without proof. That's why I brought these books from the library. Look, all different cultures from the Inuit to the Chinese have various philosophies about this matter! It *is* possible. And I am going to prove it to you. Tonight."

"I think it's a fantastic idea." Arvand replied. "But where will you go?"

"Easy. Cambridge. I am going to go to meet with Sir Isaac Newton, the world's most renowned physicist. And then I'll see what I can learn."

"HA! You, Isaac, tonight? I'll meet up with you right after I join Abraham Lincoln for soft serve," Myah scoffed.

"Um, that's Sir Isaac to you, missy," Olivia responded. "Well, whatever you cuckoos decide to do, make sure you record everything in our notebook…On the one-in-a-million chance that it actually works, we are going to need some pretty solid data to support our findings. And of course, good luck to you," Myah said laughingly, but her eyes told a more serious story.

Ding, Ding . . .Marjanah heard her mother sounding the dinner bell off their back porch in the distance. "KHR, meeting logged, 2 November, 5:49PM. Over and Out."

As the kids scrambled to gather their belongings, Arvand shoved the blanket in his backpack and Myah grabbed the carrots. In less than one minute, they brushed past the fir trees and broke into a full on run until they became little specks moving like shadowy fireflies through the dusky field.

CHAPTER 5

THE JOURNEY

Before bed, Marjanah grabbed her STEAM notebook. She knew that before she could start her experiment, she needed to have a hypothesis. Sitting crisscross applesauce on her bed, she pushed her glasses up her nose and rested the notebook on her knees.

Granted, the glasses were not technically "prescription" lenses. But they were large and very scientific looking. Marjan (her less than favorite family nickname) was convinced that wearing them made people take her more seriously and helped her figure things out more quickly. She grabbed the lucky pencil she always kept on her nightstand, in case she had an epiphany in a dream.

Name: Marjanah Jalali (why oh why did my parents have to name me after my great great grandmother?)

Hypothesis: most likely predict that A.P. will not work. If I am able to make it work, I predict being able to hover a little bit over my body, like I have seen people do in movies after they have been in an accident or something...science is real and very far from the hokey pokey stuff Olivia seems convinced has a place in our conversations...ok here goes.

Marjanah carefully slid her pencil into the spiral rings of her notebook, leaving it open to her experimental notes page, dog-eared and all, and gingerly slipped it beneath her mattress. She carefully took off her glasses, closed them and put them atop her nightstand, just beside the ice water her dad delivered at bedtime.

One more glance out the window at the dark houses across

the street. *Nothing wagered, nothing earned,* she thought determinedly as she blew her big orange cat a kiss and clicked off the lamp on her nightstand.

She lay under her blue polka dot covers and squeezed her eyes shut. *Ok Marjan, you can do this.* She pursed her lips and gripped the covers of her bed. *Nothing,* she thought. She let out a deep sigh and gazed out of the window next to her bed.

She knew when she would have to report back to KHR that her experiment had failed. *Oh well, at least I tried.* But then she remembered all the research she had done at the library. She rolled over to grab her KHR STEAM notebook from under the mattress.

Ah ha! She felt its dog-eared edge, tugged on it ever so slightly so that it was just dangling in between her two fingers and with a flip of the wrist sat up in bed like a ninja.

As she held her flashlight up by her face, she began thumbing through the pages of notes. *As I recall,* she thought, *the Inuit interpretation of Astral Projection requires the participant to be in a soft sleep. Well, how on Earth am I supposed to get from a soft sleep into the Astral Plane?!* She knew just then she had to summon the bravery of her great science heroes…On Einstein! On Curie! On Newton! And then the strangest thing happened…She closed her eyes and somewhere in the glistening world between waking and sleep she felt a sudden click, then a grab and then a whoosh—a poof—she was gone! It started slowly, so slowly. And then, just like that with the snap of some giant mystical invisible fingers, it got faster and faster. Stars exploded all around her as she was suddenly being pulled along.

And then kaPOW!

Strung out like a rock in a catapult, colors whizzing past streaks of green, then blue, then purple, gold and silver. So many shiny shiny **shiiiny** things! Marjanah was all at once not herself and yet not *not* herself either. It felt like she was bungee jumping through the universe. And then—darkness.

Whooooooooooooooooooooshhhhh*thud.*

Nothing.

CHAPTER 6

...CAMBRIDGE?

There was some very unfun prickly thing poking into Marjanah's side. "Noooo, mama I'm not ready to wake up!" she said, rolling over. She opened her eyes. "What? Oh my.....! What is this? Where am I?" The ground was hard and dirty beneath her. Twigs and leaves stuck out in all directions.

This is highly unusual, Marjanah thought, as she realized that her glasses were just barely resting on her nose. They felt thinner and lighter than her usual glasses, though. She took them off to examine them. They were small and round, with a metal frame that had large hoops to ring around your ears.

Fascinating!

In the midst of the brush, she looked down to assess the damage of what must surely have been a successful projection through the Astral Plane. She was no longer in her kitty cat pajamas with fuzzy socks. She was now wearing a fine tweed coat with two buttons across the front, a skirt that went down to her knees, and thick gray woolen tights?

Double Fascinating!

She used both hands to push herself up, like an opposite ninja, and she crawled through the bush she was apparently in and found herself on a sidewalk. There were trimmed bushes all around. Many young people wearing clothes similar to her own walked by, some laughing as they talked, some with their heads buried in books. Large stone buildings surrounded her.

The sky was grey with clouds hanging low. Rain was imminent. Some of the buildings had beautiful green ivy climbing along their walls. Marjanah listened carefully as two young people walked past her. "Well, chap that's hardly anything to fret over. A two on your final exam, at least at Cambridge, will keep you in the top quartile!"

Cambridge. She took both her

index fingers and cleaned her ears. *Cambridge? Doth my ears deceiveth me?! I made it. I. Made. It. Now I just have to find Sir Isaac Newton!*

Strapped across Marjanah's back was a small leather pack, with, by golly, her STEAM notebook tied tight to it. Even the notebook had changed. Once spiral-bound and covered with designs, it was now small and made of leather. She found a pencil in the pack and immediately began writing.

Astral Projection achieved. Appear to have traveled through time and space. Currently on Cambridge Campus, England, United Kingdom.

Clothing has changed. No longer in ~~cat pajamas~~ regular clothes. Tweed jacket with buttons, new wire-rimmed glasses. Grey woolen tights. What appears to be witch boots on feet.

Slap!

Marjanah's pencil went flying to the sidewalk. "Ouch, excuse me!"

A bicycle had stopped just short of knocking Marjanah onto the ground. "Ah, I'm sorry young lady. I am in quite a rush to meet a professor. Please excuse me," a young woman with dark hair and even deeper darker eyes explained as she stepped off her bike to help Marjanah collect her pencil.

"That's okay, I suppose." Marjanah replied. *Be brave* she thought, *get to Newton.*

She bit her lip, pausing for a second and then said "Excuse me, ma'am but I am looking to meet with Sir Isaac Newton. I have a few pressing inquiries for him."

"Ha! My dear girl. What a spritely sense of humor escapes you! You must mean you are looking for the Newton archives in the library. I can absolutely assist you in finding them."

"You mean… this is not Cambridge?"

"But *of course,* it is, that's why we have the work of world-famous scientist Isaac Newton saved in our library."

"So, what I am hearing you say is, Sir Isaac Newton is not currently teaching here?" Marjanah asked, pointing at the ground awkwardly, as if here could be anywhere other than directly where she was standing.

"My dear girl," the woman responded rather curtly, "you are either quite the little humorist or you are grossly mistaken. I shall suffer neither possibility gladly! Newton has neither taught here nor has he lived on this green Earth, let alone *here,"* She said, taking her turn to point awkwardly to the ground, "for hundreds of years!"

Knowing she had to at least begin to *appear* to make sense, Marjanah quickly regained her bearings. "Right, of course, uhm...indubitably! So. . .so. . .what is the year and date today?" she asked, bringing her sheepish gaze up from her black boots to meet the dark-haired woman before her.

"The date today is November 3rd, 1940 my dear girl. Now, might I ask where your governess is? It is highly unusual to see such a small girl, though professional enough in appearance, wandering about campus, emerging from shrubbery and such," the woman said, staring directly into Marjanah's eyes.

"Well, ahm, so you see...*think, Marjanah, THINK!* I am a student, err pupil, yes, that's it! From America. I am here doing a research project on Isaac

Newton."

The woman paused for one moment, as if determining the truthfulness of what Marjanah had just told her. "Very good then. We must get you to the library at once. I am on my way to go see a very famous scientist give a lecture. Her name is Adrienne Weill. She even worked for Madame Curie! And one must never be late. Now tell me your name dear child, and we shall be off."

"It's Marjanah, ma'am. Marjanah Jalali. Junior Scientist at your service," she said with a slight curtsey. *That's what British people did, right?* she thought grimacing to herself, nearly tripping as she tried to untangle her legs.

"Very well then, Marjanah. My name is Rosalind Franklin and you may call me just that. I would be happy to escort you to the library on my way to lecture." Rosalind began to walk at a quick clip with her bicycle alongside her, Marjanah already scrambling to keep up.

CHAPTER 7

ROSALIND

"Miss Rosalind Franklin, ma'am!" Marjanah called out nearly short of breath for the speed at which the woman in a long dark skirt, with even longer dark hair falling over her shoulders was walking. "Could you please slow down? My legs are much smaller than yours indeed!"

"Very well then child. But I must encourage you to play sports. When I was a scholar at St. Paul's, we all played hockey, cricket and of course tennis. Keeps the blood pumping, it does! Now tell me, what kind of science is it that you study?" she asked as they walked through the falling leaves of the campus green toward the library.

"Well, Ms. Rosalind, I am in a study group called KHR, err, Kids Have Rights. We perform experiments and record observations. But I personally like to study animals and plants. I want to study the Earth and make the planet a better place. What do you study, Ms. Rosalind?"

"Ah, well I am so glad to meet a young lady scientist. I myself, well I am interested in the study of life. I would like to understand how we humans grow and pass on our similarities and differences to each other. But more specifically, I am curious about the teeny tiny particles that dictate those decisions. I am going to go learn more about those particles right now!" Rosalind said excitedly.

They arrived at the steps of what appeared to be an enormous clock tower made of bricks, with long windows on either side.

"Well, my darling girl, it has been a pleasure to speak with you. Here we are at the library. Remember to continue your studies and work hard despite any obstacles you will inevitably face. The world needs more girls like you."

Marjanah met her gaze directly. "Thank you, Ms. Franklin. Thank you for walking with me and explaining your work. It has been a real honor."

"Anytime, darling!" Rosalind said, mounting her bike. "Remember to keep experimenting until your data are solid!" she said, her voice beginning to trail off already as she rode down the path, disappearing through the large trees covered in brown and burgundy leaves.

As Marjanah turned and began to walk up the stairs to the library entrance, she felt someone tug at her jacket. "Hey! What do you think you're…" she said turning around. There was no one there. *Strong wind today, hm?* She thought, trying to soothe her nerves.

TUGGG*GGGG*. This time she was flung back down the steps, nearly landing flat on her bottom.

Ahhhhhh! The chord! She knew at once that her time was up.
And then...
FLAAAAAAAAAAAAAAAAAAAA AAAAAAAAAAAP!

Off she was like a rocket, back back back. Whiteness. Falling through nothing with quick zips and zaps and lots of whizzing light. And then. Soft breezes. And then, again.

Nothing.

CHAPTER 8

BACK TO REALITY...

"Get off me...get **off** me!" she cried, pushing her covers away from her face. And with a jolt, Marjanah sat up in bed, straight like a pole. She looked around her, and reflexively grabbed her glasses off of her nightstand. "HOME!" she shouted. *I cannot believe it worked. Myah will never believe me.*

Marjanah reached for the old dog-eared spiral and pulled it up.

Astral Projection **successful.** Landed (is that the right word?) in Cambridge, England at the University. Date was November 1940. I met the most fascinating student, Rosalind Franklin. Said she was going to a lecture, interested in studying where life comes from.

<u>Note to self:</u> look up Rosalind Franklin.

Marjanah's space and time travel had made her incredibly fatigued. As soon as she set down her pencil, she fell like a tree flat onto her pillow and was snoring loudly within moments, her big clear glasses gently atop her face.

Marjanah finally began to regain consciousness as the rising sun crept into her room. She blinked and rolled over. Surely last night had been the product of too many gummy worms and not enough water. Surely it had been some kind of crazy dream. Another world? Unlikely! Time travel? Impossible!

And yet, what was this? Her journal lay open on the floor next to her bed. She flopped over like a seal and reached down to grab it. Just, one, page, she thought and pulled the old journal up and onto the bed.

Lo and behold; there it was, the name spelled out: Rosalind Franklin.

CHAPTER 9

TO THE LIBRARY!

Marjanah rolled out of bed and traded her pajamas for her favorite pair of leggings and soft, sparkly boots. She threw on a long sweater and grabbed her glasses and notebook off of her bureau. Gently placing her glasses atop her nose, she grabbed her purple backpack and raced out her bedroom door, skipping her way down the stairs.

"Marjan, breakfast!" her mom called out as she galloped through the house like a horse. "No time, Mama, gotta hit the stacks, STAT!" she laugh/called to her mom. Quick thinking as always her mom threw an apple and a yogurt pouch into Marjanah's book bag. "Marjan, please be home by noon. Jaddah and Jadd, your grandparents, are coming over and are dying to see their darling girl." "Of course, Mama, I will be back. For now-- science calls!" And with that she ran out through the mudroom, hopped on her bike and was off like a flash.

The library was open, and a few children were gathered in the children's section full of big cushions and a fish tank and lots of stuffed animals. Marjanah approached Ms. Anderson, the librarian, right away. Ms. Anderson smiled and waved. Her long blond hair flowed like water over her navy polka dot dress. "Good morning Ms. Anderson! Here on research. Can you help me find information on..." she grabbed her journal from her backpack and flipped it open to her notes page "…on Rosalind Franklin?"

"I would be thrilled Marjanah. She is one of my favorite scientists. In fact, I have the perfect book all about her in my office. Let me get it for you." Ms. Anderson was Marjanah's favorite librarian. She had huge blue eyes like two moons and wavy blonde hair she was always sloppily tying into a pony tail or bun or some other thing just to be out of her face while she read.

She helped Marjanah and deep deep down Marjanah just knew she believed in her too.

As soon as Ms. Anderson

returned with the book, Marjanah grabbed for it hungrily, whispered a quick "thank you!!" and headed off to her favorite reading nook.

CHAPTER 10

JADD KNOWS BEST

At 11:49 Marjanah packed up her book bag, still in complete shock, apple and yogurt untouched. *I cannot believe it. I simply cannot!* she thought, as she made her way past the globe carpet and the statue of the Cat in the Hat. She stopped briefly to rub his foot – for good luck of course – and headed out to the bike rack.

As she got on her bike, she thought of Rosalind. *She was one of the world's most famous scientists! She helped discover DNA, which passes traits down from generation to generation, like Myah's eyesight and my thick dark hair. But those other scientists looked at her work before she was ready to show it to anyone! That Watson and Crick! They didn't even ask to see it...grrr...*

The faster she pedaled, the faster her thoughts seemed to whir around in her mind. Regardless of what had happened last night -- whether astral projection had worked, or Rosalind had come to her in a dream -- she had made an important discovery. Her "meeting" with Rosalind must have happened to her for a reason.

Her tires came to an abrupt stop, almost leaving skid marks on her driveway as she backpedaled to break. Her grandparents' big golden boat of a car was anchored in her driveway. She had nearly forgotten they were coming. She took off her helmet and tried as best as she could to pat down her wavy black hair. She pushed her glasses up her nose, hopped off her bike and rolled it slowly into the garage.

She loved her grandparents; whom she called Jaddah for grandmother and Jadd for grandfather. She was particularly close with Jadd as he could read her like a book since she was a baby.

She coached herself, *Ok when I see Jadd and Jaddah I will be cool, calm and collected. They will have no idea what's up….just smile and nod.* But before she could make it very far, Jaddah came running. "MARJAHNAH! My darling girl you are so big!" her grandmother cried as she came rushing to her, grabbing her cheeks and enveloping her into the deep fold of her bosom for a long overdue hug.

"My darling, I have missed you," she said, grabbing Marjanah's shoulders and planting one big kiss on her forehead. A tiny cough escaped Marjanah from beneath the folds "Thanks Jaddah. Happy to see you too," she croaked.

Marjanah saw Jadd standing in the kitchen out of the corner of her eye. He smiled and gave a small wave in her direction. She made her way into the house, kicking off her fuzzy boots in the mudroom and placing her bag on the hook like her mom was always asking her to remember to do.

"Welcome home, Marjah! Now go wash up for lunch. It will be ready in 15 minutes." Her dad called from behind a pot on the stove.

Marjanah did her best invisible impression as she glided through the kitchen. But she could still feel her grandfather's eyes burning holes into the back of her sweater. She turned and ran to give him a big hug.

He knelt down to give her a

big hug. "My darling girl. What on Earth is bothering you?" he asked gently, as Marjanah's big dark eyes gazed into his. "Oh Jadd…" she began, although she was not entirely sure what to say. Somehow, she was always able to talk to her grandfather.

So just like that, the whole story unfolded out of her like a quilt. Up until that point Marjanah did not even realize herself how strange, beautiful and unfair this whole story was becoming. Then came the gentle flow of tears.

At the end of the story, Jadd looked deeply into her eyes.

"Marjahanah. This is significant. In this moment there is a lesson, but it is not I who can teach it to you. You must bring it to your friends in the KHR. I will explain to your mother why you will be late for lunch." "Oh thank you Jadd! I promise I will get everything sorted out."

And just like that, Marjanah was off to Myah's where they would call an emergency meeting of Kids Have Rights.

CHAPTER 11

SCIENCE CARNIVAL

Two weeks later, Marjanah collected the last pieces of her model DNA off of her desk. She placed them gently in the cardboard box her mom had left for her in the hallway outside of her room. She picked up the box, gave her cat one last pet and took a deep breath before heading out the door. It was time for the Winter Science Carnival.

Staring out the backseat of her dad's car, she thought about the emergency meeting of KHR they had held that night 14 days ago. At first, none of her friends believed what had happened to her. "Impossible! Absolutely ludicrous!" Myah had shouted, the squirrels practically leaping with fear from their spots in the upper branches of the fir tree.

To prove her point, Marjanah had taken the dog-eared STEAM

notebook out of her purple back pack and shown them the name her notes: Rosalind Franklin, 1940.

Marjanah presented her research from the library to the team and they slowly began to buy in. "So… what you're telling us is that she was one of the scientists who helped discover the double helix, what DNA is?" Olivia questioned.

"Yes, precisely! Except, her work was shown to other scientists before she thought it was ready. She did not live long enough to present her work, and to have maybe won a Nobel Prize with her contemporaries because she was one of the first people—and a woman no less—to photograph DNA." Marjanah explained. "I am veeeery slowly beginning to understand" Olivia smiled.

Arvand piped in, "Oliv, it's just like a computer code. DNA is the code or language for our bodies. It determines our hair and eye color and influences the ways we act and learn new things. That's why we take after our parents and ancestors. Why we are like our siblings and cousins. Rosalind helped figure out how DNA forms, but never got the big prize for it."

"Ohhhhhhhhhhh. I get it now. Yo comprehendo, gracias Arvandito." Said Olivia who was obviously practicing her very beginner's Spanish.

"I think I get where you are going with this Marjan," Myah joined. "What I hear you saying is it's time to give ole' Rosie some credit where credit is due." "Yes! This is where we right the wrong, team." Marjanah began.

"Little old us?" Olivia said mockingly, knowing full well they were capable of amazing things. "Let her talk," said Arvand, in a hushed voice.

Marjanah nodded politely at Arvand. "We are going to build a model of the double helix with a three-paneled poster including Rosalind's photograph.

We should definitely include some information on her personal history. She grew up during World War II and her family was Jewish. A lot of Jewish people were persecuted back then, many had to run and hide and millions were killed, just because of their identity. When she was a student at St. Paul's in London, she never attended church or said catholic prayers. She had to handle being different and then she still became an amazing scientist."

"It sounds like people thought she should be one way, but she chose to follow her own path. She defied expectations," Myah said in almost a whisper, staring at the pine needle carpet.

~

"Marjanah! Are you ready? We are almost at school," her mom said, snapping Marjanah out of her daze. The parking lot at Shakerside Elementary was packed.

Marjanah quickly joined up with Myah, who was arm and arm with Olivia. They waved to Arvand across the gym. They began to set up.

The competition was close, but KHR took home the blue ribbon for the second year in a row. Trina and Josh walked up to their table. "Congratulations guys. That was really interesting," Josh said, with his head a little low. "Josh is right, I loved learning about a female scientist like Rosalind Franklin. It makes me feel like I can get better at math and stuff…" Trina's voice trailed off.

"Thank you," Myah said. Olivia gave them a fake smile while Arvand high fived with Josh. "I'm super glad you learned something" Marjanah said as she fastened the blue ribbon to her sweatshirt. As Josh and Trina walked away, Myah, Olivia, Arvand and Marjanah made a circle. "All hands in," Myah said. "KHR on three!" Olivia called. The four friends yelled out "K! H! R!" and the whole gym turned to stare, as if those four ever cared if people stared at them.

"Marjanah," she heard a voice behind her say and turned quickly. To her surprise, it was Mr. Chaplan. "Uh, hi Mr. Chaplan…" she paused. "You got my name right!" she said, smiling broadly.

"Yes, er, I wanted to apologize about that, Marjanah. I also wanted to let you know what a shining star of a student you are and commend you on your amazing work at the science fair."

Myah nudged her elbow into Marjanah's side. "Thanks, Mr. Chaplan. I *am* proud of who I am and I love my name. Thanks for being our teacher, but this work reflects *all of us* at KHR."

Everyone beamed and exchanged high fives.

As Marjanah began to pack up her pieces and wave goodbye to her friends she noticed a young woman with long dark hair wearing a knee-length woolen skirt looking directly into her eyes from across the gym. She waved gracefully at Marjanah before turning on her heeled boot and leaving the double doors.

No way, Marjanah thought, *highly improbable, impossible... but* then again... *perhaps* nothing *is impossible.*

SPECIAL CONTRIBUTIONS

A special thank you to many students over the years who have inspired this book. Your endless curiosity and passion for learning lit a spark in me and I hope you continue to shine your light brightly in this world.

Thank you Caroline, my editor of many years, for your unrelenting wit and the many hours spent committed to seeing this book into creation.

Thank you Emily, for your insights and genuine, compassionate and brilliant feedback.

For the inspirational generosity and meticulous design work of Di and Ronnie—you will not be able to escape my gratitude despite what I am sure will be creative and perhaps extreme attempts.

Thank you to my parents, grandparents and ancestors for loving me and believing in me. I, along with all of my work, would not be possible without you. This is not without exclusion of *all* my family — Sally, Bill, Krissy, Alex, Andrew and of course Maria, Philip, Anna, Bennett, Arthur, Nikki, Madison and Hunter.

With profound gratitude to Spencer, the love of my life and our precious daughter, my inspiration. Spencer's research with DNA and genetics helped shape my interest in the *elemental* importance of the work and led to my interest in Rosalind Franklin.

A final note...

It is imperative that young people see the beauty and power of diversity represented in literature, and that young girls see positive role models in STEAM for their journey ahead. The world needs you. Shine your light brightly!

Made in the USA
Middletown, DE
03 June 2019